MARY STOLZ

Storm in the Night

illustrated by PAT CUMMINGS

HARPER & ROW, PUBLISHERS

For Thomas and his Cats, Alfredo & Gringo
AND
for Valrie and Robert and theirs, Mistletoes, Sir Hilary & Maché
—M. S.

For my grandfathers,
James Cummings and Robert Taylor
—P. C.

STORM IN THE NIGHT
Text copyright © 1988 by Mary Stolz
Illustrations copyright © 1988 by Pat Cummings
Printed in the U.S.A. All rights reserved.

Library of Congress Cataloging-in-Publication Data
Stolz, Mary, date.
  Storm in the night.

  Summary: While sitting through a fearsome thunder-
storm that has put the lights out, Thomas hears a
story from Grandfather's boyhood, when Grandfather
was afraid of thunderstorms.
  [1. Thunderstorms—Fiction 2. Grandfathers—
Fiction. 3. Fear—Fiction] I. Cummings, Pat, ill.
II. Title.
PZ7.S875854St 1988   [E]   85-45838
ISBN 0-06-025912-4
ISBN 0-06-025913-2 (lib. bdg.)

10 9 8 7 6 5 4 3

Storm in the night.
Thunder like mountains blowing up.
Lightning licking the navy-blue sky.
Rain streaming down the windows, babbling in
the downspouts.
And Grandfather?...And Thomas?...And
Ringo, the cat?
They were in the dark.
Except for Ringo's shining mandarin eyes and
the carrot-colored flames in the wood stove,
they were quite in the dark.
"We can't read," said Grandfather.
"We can't look at TV," said Thomas.
"Too early to go to bed," said Grandfather.
Thomas sighed. "What will we do?"
"No help for it," said Grandfather, "I shall have
to tell you a tale of when I was a boy."

Thomas smiled in the shadows.

It was not easy to believe that Grandfather had once been a boy, but Thomas believed it.

Because Grandfather said so, Thomas believed that long, long ago, probably at the beginning of the world, his grandfather had been a boy.

As Thomas was a boy now, and always would be.

A grandfather could be a boy, if he went back in his memory far enough; but a boy could not be a grandfather.

Ringo could not grow up to be a kangaroo, and a boy could not grow up to be an old man.

And that, said Thomas to himself, is that.

Grandfather was big and bearded.
Thomas had a chin as smooth as a peach.
Grandfather had a voice like a tuba.
Thomas's voice was like a penny whistle.
"I'm thinking," said Thomas.
"Ah," said Grandfather.
"I'm trying to think what you were like when you were my age."
"That's what I was like," said Grandfather.
"What?"
"Like someone your age."
"Did you look like me?"
"Very much like you."
"But you didn't have a beard."
"Not a sign of one."
"You were short, probably."
"Short, certainly."
"And your voice. It was like mine?"
"Exactly."
Thomas sighed. He just could not imagine it. He stopped trying.
He tried instead to decide whether to ask for a new story or an old one.

Grandfather knew more stories than a book full
of stories.

Thomas hadn't heard all of them yet, because he
kept asking for repeats.

As he thought about what to ask for, he listened
to the sounds of the dark.

Grandfather listened too.

In the house a door creaked. A faucet leaked.

Ringo scratched on his post, then on
Grandfather's chair.

He scratched behind his ear, and they could hear
even that.

In the stove the flames made a fluttering noise.

"That's funny," said Thomas. "I can hear better
in the dark than I can when the lights are on."

"No doubt because you are just listening," said
his grandfather, "and not trying to see and hear
at the same time."

That made sense to Thomas, and he went on
listening for sounds in the dark.

There were the clocks.
The chiming clock on the mantel struck the hour of eight.
Ping, ping, ping, ping, ping, ping, ping, ping-a-ling.
The kitchen clock, very excited.
Tickticktickticktickticktickery.
There were outside sounds for the listening, too.
The bells in the Congregational church rang through the rain.
Bong, bong, bong, bong, bong, bong, bong, BONG!
Automobile tires swished on the rain-wet streets.
Horns honked and hollered.
A siren whined in the distance.

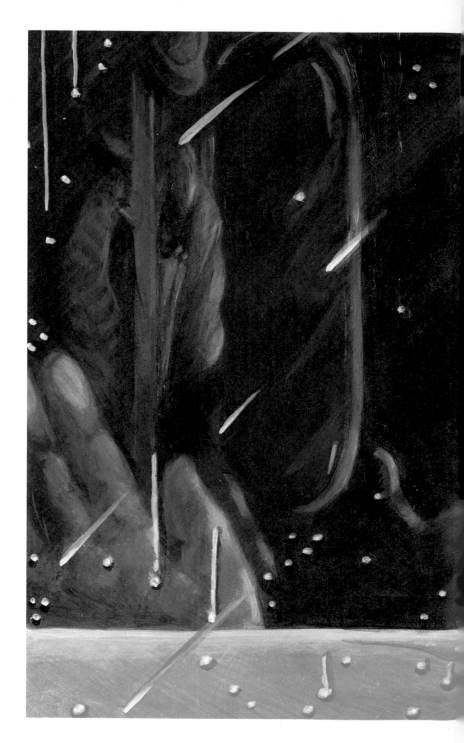

"Grandfather," said Thomas, "were there
automobiles when you were a boy?"
"Were there *automobiles*!" Grandfather shouted.
"How old do you think I am?"
"Well…" said Thomas.
"Next thing, you'll be asking if there was
electricity when I was your age."
"Oh, Grandfather!" said Thomas, laughing.
After a while he said, "Was there?"
"Let's go out on the porch," said Grandfather.
"There's too much silliness in here."
By the light of the lightning they made their way
to the front door and out on the porch.
Ringo, who always followed Thomas, followed
him and jumped to the railing.

The rain, driving hard against the back of the
house, was scarcely sprinkling here.

But it whooped windily through the great beech
tree on the lawn, brandishing branches, tearing
off twigs.

It drenched the bushes, splashed in the birdbath,
clattered on the tin roof like a million tacks.

Grandfather and Thomas sat on the swing,
creaking back and forth, back and forth, as
thunder boomed and lightning stabbed across
the sky.

Ringo's fur rose, and he turned his head from
side to side, his eyes wide and wild in the flashes
that lit up the night.

The air smelled peppery and gardeny and new.

"That's funny," said Thomas. "I can smell
better in the dark, too."

Thomas thought Grandfather answered, but he couldn't hear, as just then a bolt of lightning cracked into the big beech tree. It ripped off a mighty bough, which crashed to the ground. This was too much for Ringo. He leaped onto Thomas's lap and shivered there.

"Poor boy," said Thomas. "He's frightened."

"I had a dog when I was a boy," said Grandfather. "He was so scared of storms that I had to hide under the bed with him when one came. He was afraid even to be frightened alone."

"*I'm* not afraid of *anything*," Thomas said, holding his cat close.

"Not many people can say that," said Grandfather. Then he added, "Well, I suppose anybody could *say* it."

"I'm not afraid of thunderstorms, like Ringo and your dog. What was his name?"

"Melvin."

"That's not a good name for a dog," Thomas said.

"I thought it was," Grandfather said calmly. "He was my dog."

"I like cats," said Thomas. "I want to own a
tiger!"

"Not while you're living with me," said
Grandfather.

"Okay," Thomas said. "Is there a story about
Melvin?"

"There is. One very good one."

"Tell it," Thomas commanded. "Please,
I mean."

"Well," said Grandfather, "when Melvin and I
were pups together, I was just as afraid of storms
as he was."

"No!" said Thomas.

"Yes," said Grandfather. "We can't all be brave
as tigers."

"I guess not," Thomas agreed.

"So there we were, the two of us, hiding under
beds whenever a storm came."

"Think of that..." said Thomas.

"That's what I'm doing," said Grandfather.

"Anyway, the day came when Melvin was out on
some errand of his own, and I was doing my
homework, when all at once, with only a rumble
of warning...

down came the rain, *down* came the lightning, and all around and everywhere came the thunder."

"Wow," said Thomas. "What did you do?"

"Dove under the bed."

"But what about Melvin?"

"I'm *coming* to that," said Grandfather. "What-about-Melvin is what the story is *about*."

"I see," said Thomas. "This is pretty exciting."

"Well—it was then. Are you going to listen, or keep interrupting?"

"I think I'll listen," said Thomas.

"Good. Where was I?"

"Under the bed."

"So I was. Well, I lay there shivering at every clap of thunder, and I'm ashamed to say that it was some time before I even remembered that my poor little dog was all by himself out in the storm."

Thomas shook his head in the dark.

"And when I did remember," Grandfather went on, "I had the most awful time making myself wriggle out from under the bed and go looking for my father or my mother—to ask them to go out and find Melvin for me."

"Grandfather!"

"I told you I was afraid. This is a true story you're hearing, so I have to tell the truth."

"Of course," said Thomas, admiring his grandfather for telling a truth like *that*. "Did you find them?"

"I did not. They had gone out someplace for an hour or so, but I'd forgotten. Thomas, fear does strange things to people...makes them forget everything but how afraid they are. You wouldn't know about that, of course."

Thomas stroked his cat and said nothing.

"In any case," Grandfather went on, "there I was, alone and afraid in the kitchen, and there was my poor little dog alone and afraid in the storm."

"What did you *do*?" Thomas demanded. "You didn't *leave* him out there, did you, Grandfather?"

"Thomas—I put on my raincoat and opened the kitchen door and stepped out on the back porch just as a flash of lightning shook the whole sky and a clap of thunder barreled down and a huge man *appeared* out of the darkness, holding Melvin in his arms!"

"Whew!"

"That man was seven feet tall and had a face like a crack in the ice."

"Grandfather! You said you were telling me a true story."

"It's true, because that's how he looked to me. He stood there, scowling at me, and said, 'Son, is this your dog?' and I nodded, because I was too scared to speak. 'If you don't take better care of him, you shouldn't have him at all,' said the terrible man. He pushed Melvin at me and stormed off into the dark."

"Gee," said Thomas. "That wasn't very fair. He didn't know you were frightened too. I mean, Grandfather, how old were you?"

"Just about your age."

"Well, some people my age can get pretty frightened."

"Not you, of course."

Thomas said nothing.

"Later on," Grandfather continued, "I realized that man wasn't seven feet tall, or even terrible. He was worried about the puppy, so he didn't stop to think about me."

"Well, *I* think he should have."

"People don't always do what they should, Thomas."

"What's the end of the story?"

"Oh, just what you'd imagine," Grandfather said carelessly. "Having overcome my fear enough to forget myself and think about Melvin, I wasn't afraid of storms anymore."

"Oh, good," said Thomas.

For a while they were silent.

The storm was spent. There were only flickers of lightning, mutterings of thunder, and a little patter of rain.

"When are the lights going to come on?"
Thomas asked.

"You know as much as I do," said Grandfather.

"Maybe they won't come on for hours," said
Thomas. "Maybe they won't come on until
tomorrow!"

"Maybe not."

"Maybe they'll *never* come on again, and what
will we do then?"

"We'll think of something," said Grandfather.

"Grandfather?"

"Yes, Thomas?"

"What I think...I think that maybe if you
hadn't been here, and Ringo hadn't been here,
and I was all alone in the house and there was a
storm and the lights went out and didn't come on
again for a long time, like this...I think maybe
then I would be a *little* bit afraid."

"Perfectly natural," said Grandfather.

Thomas sighed.

Grandfather yawned.

Ringo jumped to the porch floor and walked
daintily into the garden, shaking his legs.

After a while the lights came on.

They turned them off and went to bed.